friends to lovers to exes and what's next?

A Romantic Tragedy

by Hugo Jepsen

AF440487

Preface

The question, *'friends to lovers to exes and what's next?'* came to me as some sort of epiphany late at night.

I, immediately, reached out to my friends about this; they just laughed at me, for a short while, and asked me, *'are you serious? why would you want to care about what's next with an ex?'*. I don't know yet, but what happens next?

I have always believed that people come into our lives for a reason and leave for other reasons; however, what's that supposed to mean? My anxiety keeps asking me – 'what's next?' – for the most part of my life; I always wonder about the future with too much anxiety, especially when people come into the mix.

In this book, I've attempted to select a few poems written on the subject. I hope you enjoy it!

The Kindle Version only contains 8 poems. The Paperback Version contains the 8 original poems intended for this book with 12 extra as exclusive poems.

Chapters:

Paperback Exclusive Chapters:

1. love you crazy this way
2. overthink way too much
3. don't say goodbye
4. swimming in passion
5. but we were
6. wishing that I had stayed
7. these arms of mine
8. old messages
9. touching the sky
10. we will be
11. killing me tonight
12. hoax

friends to lovers to exes and what's next?

What does it mean to you to be my friend?
You and I shared the same bed,
and we've broken each other's hearts,
and now, you've become my ex.

There's something I don't understand —
You come and go, go hot and cold,
it's driving me to my own edge,
lies or truths to make me get sold.

Yet, there's something I know —
it might not be now or ever,
but you grow closer when you lose
and you've lost it —me and you, together.

But, are you still capable of love?
I might've changed, I might not be,
and there are seven billion in the world
and so —are you able to choose me?

green branches

The green branches of olive trees
are growing themselves to
pierce their roots inside of me —
what am I supposed to do?

The semblance of the shade
and the yearning they utterly make
and the gripping sound
that I hear whenever they break.

And they've broken out
inside a body that is mine —
all the words they tell me about
are about tipping points in time.

They've pierced through
and we've become one —
the way that I feel the world
is the way that we've become —
and baby, it burns, I feel it burn.

hug the roots of a tree

Hug the roots
of a single tree
if you ever need me.

Put your head up to the sky
to just let the rain
touch your face
when you want to wash your pain away.

And let the sun burn
the depths of your heart
to let yourself free
for you and me, to restart.

it's overflowing, help me

If I pinch my bubble
it will overflow —
I can feel it all,
especially in my soul.

There's so much I'd like to
talk about but only with you.
You've got your eyes around,
and there's nothing I can do.

But if I suppress this for too long,
maybe, they'll disappear one day —
but what if it doesn't happen
exactly, exactly, that way?

There's a kaleidoscope of colours
pouring out rainbows for me
but I don't seem interested
in being happy, in being free.

I keep going around in circles
with no answers but no requests,
just a strong wish for it all to be
alright with no life force left for it.

my anxiety is killing our relationship

I carved in a tree, your name,
so my heart can find a stable ground
when your passion makes me feel insane.

You've given up the heaven above,
so you could save me from the hell that I live in -
if that is not love — what then? what is love?

I just want to live in this moment forever,
but I'm afraid if I don't get any better,
I'll be missing out on us being together.

And I apologize for all the mistakes,
my anxiety is destroying our relationship —
and I can't only see it, I can feel it too.
Would you forgive me? Would you?

glitch in time

Another attempt, another try,
wanted love but only found lust —
another meeting with friends,
more drinks, another club.

My mother told me to be
the most reckless boy
they have ever seen —
if to played as a toy
is what I don't want for me.

Yet, another try, another attempt,
wanted lust, but this time, found love —
I hope that, for now, it is good enough.

Summer nights have arrived,
holding hands under the moon —
I think I found a glitch in time.

holding you in the future

I never get to hold you
as long as I want to —
time passes by quickly
when we both never do.

Until I see you standing
in the midst of my thunderstorm,
I'm fine with staying in your arms.

If nobody ever understands
when you speak about love —
I hope to make sure that
what you speak is enough.

I never get to hold you tight,
but someday, in the future,
I hope to hold you as mine.

it's probably for the best

It's probably for the best
to rest when I feel tired —
it's more likely to address
a situation without ever having tried.

But what pains me in this story
is that, I haven't found the maturity
to understand what's in my heart —
I thought I grew up, but I just did start.

love you crazy this way

I want to love you again
like I have not done
for any other man
that I've ever met.

You make me feel like I'm number two,
but I know, I might be falling for you,
because I think about you every second,
and I ask myself, 'does it really matter?'.

I gotta get out of my head
that only makes me sad,
I should've listened to my heart,
right there, from the very start.

I know I ran away,
I know there's nothing,
nothing I can do or say,
but make me love you crazy this way.

overthink way too much

I can't say I'm fine,
I can't fake I'm alright,
I know we're short on time,
but for three weeks, be mine.

Just mine, all for myself,
I wonder if that's selfish
or if I want to love just like everyone else.

Maybe, I'm needy for you,
Maybe, I need you around,
or maybe, I'm just a fool,
but maybe, just for now.

I'm happy for all the love
because I don't feel like I deserve,
that I deserve to be enough,
but maybe, I overthink way too much.

don't say goodbye

You hurt me
and I hurt you,
You're in love
and I love you too.

Some things
are not meant to last
but lying is too hard
because the truth is hard to ask.

We should hug each other,
we should tell pretty lies,
use each other one more time,
one last night, just one last night.

Let's forget about it all,
and just for tonight,
let's delay the fall
with no goodbyes.

swimming
in passion

I wish you were here now,
and I wish I could close my eyes
but if you want to understand me,
baby, just look at the sky.

Unlock the gate so I can leave,
wash way the fire you put in me,
and please, make me believe
that I'm your everything.

All I want is to lose myself in you,
but it's hard to know the truth,
and it's hard to make any promises
if all lies are what I'm going through.

I wish I could find a way
to tell you all I want to say,
but baby, my heart is so thin
and you should know I can't swim.

but we were

Love, love has to win
without a question mark.
I don't know where we've been,
but we were there from the start.

Truth, the truth found us all,
we were about to break
but we were saved from the fall
by the love, we were able to create.

Lies, the lies were always bulletproof,
never hidden from the truth,
we just kept on with our lives
without lies covering our eyes.

Friends, lovers from now on,
one day, we'll look back in time,
and we'll just wish, just wish
we never said goodbye.

wishing that I had stayed

You should know
that I had no choice,
my heart is as soft
as the words of my voice.

But now, I listen to none,
all I wanted is pure fun,
and all I want for now
is for us to go deep down.

I'm going to be the end,
the end of the world,
and if you get cold,
I'll be your warmth.

And one day,
you'll wake up
wishing that,
that I had stayed.

these arms
of mine

Let's forget about the pain,
the pain attached to my name,
otherwise, we'll just be repeating
the old same mistakes.

Let's hold our hands one more time
and everything will be perfect,
I promise you, all will be alright.

I promise I won't run,
I'll find my way back to you,
I won't let the fire of the sun
stop me from loving you.

When you look up to the night sky
you need to pay attention to the moon
to remember the shape of my eyes.

Call for me at the edge of the night,
I need to tell you, you'll be safe,
safe in these arms of mine.

old messages

Reading old messages
is like living in old memories
and for once, we were a dream
and I was the star of your film.

Everything has to change
between time and place,
but something I never lost,
I never lost my grace.

I keep being the same,
I keep wandering in love,
I keep wanting fortune and fame,
but nothing for me is ever enough.

And once you leave, I'll disappear
like the bad lover that I am,
and that's not the kind of man
that I want to be,
that's just not me.

touching the sky

For a moment, for a second,
we felt like touching the sky,
we felt like grains of sand
and we don't know why.

We were one, we were,
we always want to
be more and more.

We were the stars,
we cared and we care,
from the very start.

For an hour or two,
the only thing we can tell you
is that we were left in paradise
and don't wake us up,
don't open your eyes.

we will be

Of course, I feel too much,
my heart is full of love,
love to give and take,
the love I can only create.

Go on and live your life,
I'm not running out,
not running out of time,
at least, not for now.

Go on, be with whoever,
by the end, we'll be together,
we are the kind of light
that will never stop to ignite.

Everybody wants to go fast
and get stabbed at the back,
but I just want to be with you,
and we will be, we will be true.

killing me tonight

It hurts me so much within,
I just feel my heart getting thin,
and I feel a stroke inside of me,
I want to get out of me, away with it.

I feel some rainbows for real,
but I never accepted such a deal,
I feel some gold in your touch
but it was never, ever enough.

I feel some passion inside my bones,
but it was never really shown,
and I feel your warmth at night
even if you're sleeping outside.

And all the memories kept above
are coming back so strong this time
that all I feel now is just love
and that love is killing me tonight.

hoax

If you can't sleep at night,
it's because I'm screaming
your name to the sky.

If you can't be awake,
it's because I'm here
dreaming about your face.

If I can't hold my tears,
hold me tight,
and understand my fears.

But if I die for you,
don't cry about it.
It will be about love
and I'll be looking to,
to you from above.

Credits

Writer: Hugo Jepsen
Editor: Hugo Jepsen
Cover Creator: Hugo Jepsen
Image License: Unsplash
Publisher: Amazon

Disclaimer

Any resemblance to other creative projects is mere coincidence.

Copyrights

Protected and Licensed with a Copyright Infringement.